IRISH CAR BOMB

BY

C.S. ANDERSON

BOOK THREE OF
THE BLACK IRISH CHRONICLES

This, the final volume in THE BLACK IRISH
CHRONICLES, is dedicated to our readers,
backers, supporters and fans. Starting our own
small press and releasing these books has been an
amazing rollercoaster ride of an adventure and
would not have been possible without all of you.
Thank you all for riding along on the adventures of
Joe Gunn and crew. This series has ended but stay
tuned for more releases from Alucard Press!

Alucard Press 2014

CHAPTER ONE

Brain and I charge up the path leading to the house, both of us carrying H&K MP5 submachine guns full of blessed hollow points at the ready. My senses detect no nearby vampires or Renfields but my instincts tell me we may already be too late.

We left you a present in the kitchen...

That is what the clearly vampire voice had said over the phone, the phone that there should have been no damn way on earth that anyone outside of The Order should have access to the number for.

The phone had gone dead right after that.

The door to the house stood wide open, not a good sign.

I gesture for Brain to slow down, we move in carefully because this has all the earmarks of a trap. Any manner of ambush or booby traps could be waiting past the door and probably were.

We had left a heavily armed Keela and Jenny in that house. The house should have been safe, well as safe as any place could be now with the Banshee/Vampire war raging in the shadows all around us. The house sat on what was supposed to be hallowed ground which should keep out vampires but wouldn't slow down Banshees, Renfields or determined Dark Adepts.

That was the problem with being on everyone's shit list, trouble could come from any direction.

As my old mentor had been fond of saying, "Opportunity knocks but trouble just kicks the damn door in."

And as we come through the doorway I see this to be literally true. The door has been bashed in and hung crookedly on its busted hinges.

We left you a present in the kitchen...

Together we creep down the long dark hallway, Brain snakes out a hand tries the light switches but of course they are out. Fanning out he takes the left side and I take the right. I am using every sense and instinct, human and otherwise that I have and they tell me that the house is empty but I have been wrong before.

And paid the bloody price.

I give him a nod and Brain flips on the tactical flashlight on his weapon and I do the same. Together we move quickly down the hall that leads into the kitchen, the flashlights casting cones of light ahead of us and creating crazy funhouse shadows.

The kitchen is a fucking slaughter house, blood is just every damn where. Even dripping down from the ceiling in a slow obscene mockery of gentle rain. I glance around and take in three dead Renfields and a couple of butchered newbie vampires in one corner and a dead Banshee and three slaughtered Dark Adepts complete with blood drenched black robes in another. The floor is littered with spent shell casings.

Seems everyone was invited to this party.

We left you a present in the kitchen....

They left her on the kitchen table, on display. Naked and bloody, her throat so torn out that she was damn near decapitated. The flashlights unforgiving light sparing us no horrible detail.

We both take in a deep shuddering breath as the shock of it hits us. Brain sinks to his knees and a low moan begins to come from him. Feral and devastated, full of rage, loss and pain. It builds into a desperate howl that echoes wildly in the small kitchen.

My own blind rage and grief bursts from me in the same moment and just like his, mine too is a rage and sorrow filled mad howl.

Mine shatters every window in the house.

CHAPTER TWO

It also shatters the illusion wrapped around us. Suddenly the body on the table is a stranger's.

"I saw Jenny." Brain gasps as he struggles shakily to his feet.

"And I saw Keela, heads up something powerful enough to mindfuck us both without voice tricks or eye contact is here with us." I snap at him.

"I am here Black Irish." A voice says from right behind us.

We both whirl around and point guns at the vampire standing there. Something is very wrong here, my marks are quiet, but at least I can sense him a little now. He is old, older even than Martin, the Master vampire who had tried to turn me, had been. At least a thousand years old, maybe more. Tall and gaunt and impossibly slender with sharply chiseled features, he stared back at us calmly. A very old looking sword was in a scabbard on his right hip.

"Please lower your weapons, I could have killed you at any moment from the time you entered the house. I merely wish to talk. I am known as Avanticus." His voice is flat and empty.

"Why the mind games asshole?" Brain asks through clenched teeth, he carries a lot of anger inside him that he keeps on a very tight leash. Sometimes the grip on that leash is more white knuckle than others, this is one of those times.

"I have a rare ability amongst my kind that has continued to grow stronger over the centuries. I can use such illusions to cloak my presence, instead of perceiving me you saw your worst fears realized. I apologize if you found it unsettling." There wasn't a trace of apology in the vamps voice.

Brain gets ready to say more but I flash him the hand signal to stand down and with the barest hesitation he follows it.

"Your females are unharmed, they are good warriors Black Irish, I will freely grant you that. Still, without my timely intervention they would have perished. No need to thank me I had my own reasons for doing so. I have glamoured them asleep and they will not awaken until dawn. They are upstairs in the second bedroom on the left."

I nod at Brain to go check it out and the ancient vampire and I stand staring at each other until he appears at the top of the stairs and gives me the thumbs up.

I set my gun down on the blood splattered table next to the corpse that for one awful moment I had thought was the love of my life and gesture towards the sword that the vamp was wearing.

He hesitates for a moment and then gives an eloquent shrug. Moving with deliberate, almost mocking slowness he unbuckles it and places it next to my gun.

In all my years doing this I have never met a vampire who carried a weapon, I mean hell, with their strength and speed they are fucking weapons. Like everything else going on tonight it made no sense.

"The sword isn't a weapon." I tell him flatly playing on a hunch.

"Very good, Black Irish. No indeed it is not, more of a talisman of sorts really. It serves to amplify my ability to cloak myself with illusion somewhat. Also, I have worn it for so very long that it has become a habit."

He regards me for a moment, his face like all of the ancients is so alien as to be unreadable even to me. The way he cocks his head when he looks at me is bird like especially odd since the rest of his body doesn't move at all.

"You look well, Black Irish. Recovered from your encounter with The Morrigan? Pity you and your order didn't manage to seal the breach between our world and her realm before some of her Banshee escaped. They have killed three of my progeny."

"Shit happens." I tell him gruffly.

Quite a lot of it lately really. The Order estimates that at least one hundred of the Banshee spirits made their way into our world. No clue where they pulled that number from, like all bureaucracies they had the magical power to pull numbers out of their ass when they needed them. They, as their queen mother had told us, took up shop in what she had called "The least amongst you," mostly mentally ill homeless men and women.

Once possessed they became something no longer human, we have no idea how powerful they would have been if their dark queen had followed them into our world, but as is they were formidable. The Banshee possessed humans were far stronger, faster and harder to kill than normal humans. They also had razor sharp claws that actually were capable of doing damage to their hated enemies the vampires. Their bite was also poisonous to vamps, especially the younger ones and their screeching cry seemed to physically pain the vamps.

"Indeed Black Irish. The war rages around us, we kill them and they simply flee to find a new host. It has become a war of attrition against us and I fear that we are losing ground. I have come here tonight to tell you that we will not allow this to continue. The Council is considering several measures, each harsher and more drastic than the last I fear."

The Order has had its hands full since the coming of the Banshee, their spin doctors working overtime to keep the war firmly in the shadows. Guns that once hunted killer vamps now found themselves patrolling the streets and keeping normal humans from harm. The Banshee had no specific interest in killing humans but would slaughter as many as stood between them and their targets. Collateral damage was upping the city's homicide rate.

"This house is on Holy ground, how is it that you are standing here?" I wonder out loud.

"A coven of Dark Adepts desanctified the grounds moments before tonight's follies began." There is a slight edge in his voice now, he didn't like me changing the subject.

"The Banshee are bound here, your kind is not. Why don't you simply leave? Hell deprived of a purpose the Banshee might just wither away." I tell him even though I know what his answer will be.

He does his imitation of a bird and cocks his head at me again staring at me with his dark unreadable eyes.

"There are many on the Council who believe that your Order engineered the whole encounter with The Morrigan to allow the Banshee access to this city. To force us to abandon this territory and make Seattle a vampire free zone. If we allow this here, they feel that you will simply repeat the process until you have driven us away from each major city. No, Black Irish my kind do not so lightly abandon territories. I come here this night to seek a formal meeting between the vampire

Council and your Order. A solution must be found. I am here to tell you that since the Banshee inhabit what The Morrigan so charmingly called "The least of you," one of the plans on the table is to simply wipe out the homeless population of this city. Another is to forcibly turn hundreds of humans and create a flock of newbie vampires to use as cannon fodder to distance the rest of us from this conflict." He tells me like I would tell Keela I am buying a quart of milk at the local market.

Brain and I killed a vampire just a few nights ago that we had caught slaughtering five homeless men sleeping under a freeway overpass. He had justified his action by telling us that they would have eventually been possessed and therefore a threat. We didn't buy his proactive self-defense plea so we had blown his brains out with blessed bullets.

"You must know that either of those approaches would result in all out war between us. Our White Adepts are working on a way to return the Banshee to their realm." I told him grimly.

"There are those on the Council and truth be told, in your own Order who feel that such a war is inevitable and perhaps over do. I am not amongst them. I am formally now asking for a sit down meeting with your Order, will you pass that along to your superiors?"

I nod at him and just like that he is gone, I glance at the kitchen table and the sword is gone as well. Every time I start to think that I am fast, an ancient vamp redefines the word for me.

Hate that.

I use the compromised cellphone and call for a cleanup, it has been a long night and our priority now is to get the girls safely home

The phone drops to the floor and I grind it into rubble with my boot, Keela and Jenny are alive and we all live to fight another day.

Time to go home and call that a win.

CHAPTER THREE

The girls wake up screaming and reaching for weapons that aren't there as soon as the first rays of the sunrise hit the house. We manage to calm them down and try to extract the story of the night before from them but they insist on showering the blood and gore from them and changing into clean clothes first.

Their memories are not entirely intact but slowly we pull together a rough version of last night's events. The story is told in fits and starts between the pair of them and we cobble together a timeline.

Keela had gotten a whiff of the scorched metal and rotting meat stench of dark magic just as the coven had desanctified the grounds. What their next step was meant to be, we will likely never know, because the moment they did so a group of young vamps and a few Renfields fleeing a determined pack of Banshee had spilled into the yard and a full fledge battle had broken out.

Some of the vampires were badly wounded and needed fresh blood to heal and smelling the two women in the house they had broken in and attacked.

Bad idea.

Keela and Jenny had opened fire and had a busy several minutes as the Banshee, Dark Adepts and the rest of the vamps had stormed the house. They had been gaining the upper hand when the elder vampires had shown up.

The last thing either of them remembers is a large group of very old vampires appearing in front of the house.

Fade to black.

As matter of factly as possible and leaving out our emotional devastation we told them our part of the story and our encounter with Avanticus. Keela seems sure that he must have intervened in whatever the elder vampires had shown up to do.

Jenny thinks he might have stepped in simply to gain favor with us and buy some cooperation in arranging the sit down he seems to want.

Things with the vampires, especially the elders are seldom that damn simple but anything is possible.

None of us mentions the elephant in the room, the vampires who called us had access to what was supposed to be a secure line provided by The Order. The trust between us has always been strained, even more so since the events that brought the Banshee into our world. I am just too big of a wild card for them to enjoy having me in the deck, considering all the types of power that I have been touched by. My trainee Brain once crashed their entire computer system and they know that he could likely do it again if he wanted to. Keela is more or less guilty by association. Not to mention that not so long ago my mentor, a respected and trusted member of The Order had turned traitor and turned me over to a master vampire who had wanted to turn me.

Yeah, trust issues on both sides of the fence.

Jenny looks shaken, she is a former United States Marine and tough as nails but she has been getting glimpses into our world since hooking up with Brain. She is a tough customer but fighting things that don't officially exist and almost dying is a stretch for someone who is basically a civilian. Running a bar doesn't prepare you for what we routinely do, hell neither does being a former Marine who has seen combat for that matter.

Brain sits near her and has a hand resting gently on her arm, I hate to be the one to say it but as this war heats up I don't like the odds for them having a happily ever after. Probably not a good time to go out choosing china patterns and all that.

We are dancing in the dark here, trouble is coming at us fast and hard and from all directions. Too much we don't know, obviously there is a leak in security at The Order but how high does it go? Who was the poor woman they left for us to find? Why did Avanticus intervene? What is the vampire Council's true agenda in wanting a sit down meeting with The Order? So many questions.

So few answers.

In other words, business as usual.

Fuck it, time for waffles.

One of my many talents is that I make amazing waffles. Another one of my many and varied talents is knowing when to let shit go and make waffles. This is one of those times.

"Ok kids, time for waffles!" I tell them all cheerfully.

"Seriously?" Jenny looks at me like I have completely lost my mind. Brain makes eye contact with me and catches my mood perfectly.

"Awesome idea!" He chirps standing up.

Keela comes over and puts her head on my shoulder almost undoing me, the moment when I thought that I had lost her flashes through my mind quick and ugly. I hug her to me and do my best not to burst into tears.

It sucks sometimes being a hard ass fearless vampire hunter.

"Only if that deal includes mimosas." She says quietly.

"Deal! Ok boys will makes waffles and girls will make mimosas." Brain says as he walks into the kitchen.

He walks out again a split second later with his gun in his hand.

"We've got company." He tells me tersely.

I really don't want to go see what's in the kitchen but I go anyway. Brain steps out of the way and lets me go by.

What I see is weird even for us.

There is a short Asian female vampire stretched out on the kitchen table. She is very lucky that there are no windows in the kitchen or she would be a crispy critter right about now. She has long jet black hair and is dressed head to toe in black leather, like some frat boy's wet dream version of a dominatrix. On her unmoving chest is a hand written note.

Come darkness we need to talk.

Oh, we will fucking talk all right, starting with how the hell she got in here past Brain's beyond state of the damn art security systems and then moving on to who the hell she is and what the hell she wants with us.

I back out of the kitchen and the four of us sweep the house to make sure that there aren't any more surprises. Brain checks and rechecks and then fucking checks all of his security equipment again but all of it is working perfectly. I can feel his frustration because what happened is just not possible.

Once again, business as usual.

Nothing to be done until nightfall so believe it or not we resume our plan of waffles. The girls work on the mimosas at the farthest end of the kitchen away from the vamp.

Brain stands staring down at her with a grim look on his face. I watch him carefully, I know how he feels about vampires but if he moves to kill her I will stop him. We need answers and she can't give them if he riddles her in blessed bullets or drags her outside to fry.

After a moment he reaches into his pocket and pulls out a black Sharpie marker and uses it to draw a Snidely Whiplash style mustache on her face. Stepping back to admire his handy work he flashes me a crooked grin and without being able to help it I start busting up laughing. The girls roll their eyes at us but soon they are laughing too, and just like that a good deal of the tension in the room drains away and our morning is back on track.

It's the little things.

CHAPTER FOUR

The vampire's eyes pop open just as the sun sets, if the sight of three guns pointed at her head bothers her, she shows no sign of it. As I watch, the Sharpie mustache Brain doodled on her earlier fades away and vanishes. Just as well, would have been hard having a serious conversation with her otherwise.

"My name is Janelle, my sire and Master is Avanticus. You have no need of those guns, my Master has instructed me to do you no harm and I am incapable of disobeying him." Her voice is flat but I think I can hear just a hint of resentment in it.

Now that she is awake I can read her, she is barely forty years undead which might be a problem. Newer vamps feel an almost overpowering need to feed upon awakening and nobody here is on the damn menu.

"Can you control your thirst fledgling?" I ask her harshly.

"You are in no danger my Master chose me for this particular errand because my control is flawless. After our business here is completed I have a juice box nearby that I will visit and feed upon."

A juice box is vamp slang for a human willing to be fed upon, usually for the sexual thrill of it, sometimes for money, hell sometimes for both. Unless the vamp goes overboard and kills the donor or addicts them into becoming a Renfield it is none of our business.

"How did you get in here without setting off our security systems?" Brain demands.

"My master brought me here, he is over a thousand years old, many things are possible for him that are not for other Wizards." There is an echo of pride in her voice

"So, you know his name, do you know mine?" I ask her.

"You are known as Black Irish, many stories are told of you. I thought you would be taller."

Her voice is so dry and empty that I have no idea if she is fucking with me or not.

"Ok Janelle time to play twenty questions." I tell her as I lower my gun, after a long moment everyone else but Jenny lowers theirs.

She sits up slowly and stares unblinkingly at me.

"My Master has put no set limit on the number of questions you may ask, Black Irish."

Oh yeah, she is probably a blast at parties.

I put the whole security issue on the backburner, if her Master has instructed her not to tell us, no amount of repeating the question will do any good. Vampires this new are in absolute thrall to their makers, even after they mature and grow into their powers, they still are expected to obey but there is more wiggle room.

"Why are you here Janelle?""

"In part, Black Irish, because my Master wishes me to give you a warning. Your Order much like our Council is conflicted. There are those in both groups trying to avoid war and those who would embrace it. The part of your Order that would embrace war has betrayed you. It is known that since the attack on your former home you all now rotate between houses that the Wizard owns and various safe houses. Your movements are being tracked and that information is being leaked to those who would harm you." She says this in a formal tone, obviously simply following instructions.

It makes sense, however Avanticus foxed our security systems, he did it to show that it can be done. He did it to show that we aren't safe anywhere. If it was a move to rattle us, it was working, damn it!

"Who was the woman on the table and who killed her?" I ask through clenched teeth. If I could I planned on seeking a little good old fashioned vengeance on whoever it was. Vengeance is mine sayeth the Lord, but the Lord is busy and I don't mind helping out.

"Her name was Rose Winters. She was a volunteer at one of your city's homeless shelters. Vampires who favor going to war killed her and left her there to taunt you. They had plans for your human bitches as well, but my Master, persuaded them to change those plans." There is a trace of pride in her voice.

"Why the general hard on for me? All modesty aside if I hadn't renewed the spell holding The Morrigan in her slumber, you vampires would be busy being out right exterminated about now."

"That is the position that my Master has taken with the Council. There are many who do not believe The Order's version of events. Many believe that you deliberately brought the Banshee amongst us, if not you yourself Black Irish, then your Order."

"Do you fear the Banshee?" Jenny asks, she has pulled up a kitchen chair but her gun has never wavered from being pointed at the vampire's head.

"My master has ordered me to survive any encounters I many have with them so I will strive to obey. I fear them less than I fear disobeying him. You speak of my fear, I can smell your fear human, tell me, do you really feel up to the company you are keeping?" The vamps tone is bored and she doesn't even do Jenny the courtesy of looking at her when she answers. It is as if she has already decided that Jenny is the weak link amongst us and dismissed her and I suppose that is truer than any of us want to dwell on.

For centuries The Order has kept the balance between the vampire and human worlds. We monitor the vamps and take out the one who stray over the line.

The coming of the Banshee has upset that balance and both worlds are reeling from it. If the vampires resort to the harsh measures Avanticus mentioned, we will have to respond and the hostilities will escalate to a level we will not be able to hide from the authorities. First the police and then the government will become involved and then wiping out the vampire threat becomes and all out military operation, countless human lives will be lost in the battles to come. It won't be the blood bath that The Morrigan wanted but it will be close.

That can't be allowed to happen.

Not on my watch.

"As I told your Master, we are working on a solution to the Banshee problem. We will not be the ones to start a war, but we will finish it. War will benefit no one on either side." I tell her flatly.

She tilts her head at me, the mannerism an echo of her creator. Her eyes are hard black marbles but she isn't old or strong enough to use them on me.

"I know that you have passed on my Master's request for a meeting between the vampire Council and your Order. I am to tell you that your presence at that meeting is being formally called for. You are being called to testify Black Irish."

Awesome, the supernatural equivalent to jury duty.

I nod at her to acknowledge the point and in a blink she is standing up in front of me. She stares at me for a moment and then returns the nod.

"Very well then, I must now feed. Have I your permission to leave or do you have more questions for me?" Her tone is still empty but I can hear notes of need in it now. I have a lot more questions but she likely wouldn't be allowed to answer most of them. I would rather not test her control, no matter how good she claims it is and I don't want to send her to her juice box too starved to exercise enough control not to kill.

"Tell your master you have served adequately." I tell her as I gesture towards the front door.

A hint of a smile plays across her face and moving faster than a vamp her age should have been able to, she blurs over to Jenny and takes the pistol away from her. Standing in front of her she snaps it in half and hands it back to her.

And then she is gone. Jenny sits there for a stunned moment looking at the pieces of her weapon with a lost look on her face. Brain helps her stand up and shakily she leaves the room with him.

Jenny and Brain move off to a different part of the house to talk, Keela shoots me a look that I can only respond to with a shrug. Jenny has been winding up to a freak out since she moved in and the last twenty four hours have been rough even by our standards and things show no sign of slacking off anytime soon. It is what it is.

Brain is training to be a Gun like me and I don't see him giving that up. He has seen and done too much to go out and pretend to be a civilian. If Jenny is looking for a white picket fence, two point five kids and a husband who comes home from a straight job every day, well she set her sights on the wrong guy.

They talk for a long time and then we hear the front door slam and her little Mini Cooper start up. Keela looks at me again, she is a caregiver and wants to fix everything but some things aren't ours to fix. I shake my head sadly at her telling her to let this go.

Brain comes back alone so it isn't hard doing the math about what happened.

"We are taking a break for a while, she is pretty stressed out." He tells tersely in a tone that doesn't invite interrogation.

"You ok to go out on patrol?" I ask him, though it isn't really a question. Ever since the coming of the Banshee, patrols of Guns have been covering the city trying to keep the battles from involving humans and trying to keep those battles contained to the shadows.

"Of course." He grunts.

"I am coming with tonight." Keela says firmly.

I open my mouth to protest but then think better of it and close it before I say something stupid. It is a skill I am slowly developing.

Hell, after what happened last night she is probably safer with us than here on her own. Avanticus proved that our security can be breached and has informed us that we aren't safe in any of our usual places. We will go on patrol and then find a place to lie low for a while, off the grid.

"Ok kids let's gear up then."

Hours later and we are parking behind a flooring warehouse in the SODO district. This has always been prime vampire hunting grounds because of the sizeable homeless population and the flood of drunk club goers from the handful of cool clubs in the neighborhood. It is our last sweep of the night and then we will find a random motel to crash in.

Since it is after last call the area is deserted. I take point and Keela and Brain spread out behind me. She takes the left and he takes the right and we start walking down First Avenue. We are only carrying handguns, too hard to explain to any police who might roust us why we have anything heavier. Since the rocket attack by mercenaries on Brain's old house we have tried hard to stay off of police radar. We each have a concealed permit for the guns so the cops might not like us wandering around with guns, but they wouldn't be able to do much about it.

We don't make it three blocks before trouble finds us.

A black panel van comes squealing around a corner and stops in front of us. The side doors fly open and a snarling mob of starving newbie vamps comes pouring out coming at us in a ragged charge. The van peels out and is gone in seconds.

The next few minutes we spend trying really fucking hard not to die.

Keela sticks her gun right into the mouth of the large black female vamp trying to eat her face and double taps it. She just barely has time to swing her gun to take out the scruffy bearded hipster vamp coming up on her left and she blows his brains out the back of his head with one well placed shot.

They rush us so starved that they are fearless, they are so new my scars barely tingle. I kill the first one to rush me and slam the second one into the brick wall behind me. It gets back up and lunges for my throat and it takes three to the head to put it down.

Brain has killed three but his gun is empty. A blonde teenage cheerleader vamp leaps snarling for his throat and he clubs her with his big ass revolver so hard I can hear bones in her face shatter. She goes down and he makes sure she stays down by smashing her head in with his steel toed boots.

I put my last four rounds into the biggest of them, a hulking Samoan looking vamp with a shaved head. He goes down but he is still trying to crawl towards me as I reload. Two more rounds seal the deal.

Keela puts her gun right on the forehead of the vamp trying to bite through her boots, her first two shots had taken out the things legs and it was still trying for her. She fires twice and the show is over.

Brain is leaning against a building using a speed loader to reload his revolver, he looks at me walking up to him.

"Jesus, Joe if we had been civilians we would be dead right now." He says taking deep breaths.

"That was a straight up ambush brother, whoever it was knew where we would be." I tell him grimly.

The schedule and routes for us to sweep came by encrypted email, someone had set us up.

Normally I would call for a cleanup but these vampires are so damn new that in a couple of hours any autopsy done on them will come up ordinary human.

There are already sirens in the distance, Keela gives us a pointed look and she is right, it is time to be elsewhere. We full out run, with our guns ready for more nasty surprises, back to the car. Time to find someplace totally off the grid to lay low.

Tomorrow we will force a meeting with my field officer Morton. I will be asking pointed questions that there damn well better be answers too or I will pick the little bastard up and shake those answers out of him.

It is nice to have something to look forward to.

CHAPTER FIVE

Brain used encrypted email on his tablet to set up the meet with Morton. It was at a different sketchy looking warehouse in a different not great part of town as last time but the places could have been interchangeable. None of us are in great moods, we took turns grabbing sleep at the dump of a motel we ended up in but none of us got enough.

We sit quietly for a moment and then as if by some prearranged signal we all got up and out of the car and walked to the warehouse.

As we step inside three Guns step out of the shadows, one big guy with a badly receding hairline, a skinny looking red head and a sturdily built Hispanic guy.

"Hey fellas! Is Morty around?" Brain chirps at them with a mocking smile.

"Watch your mouth trainee." The big guy snaps at him as he swings a backhanded slap at him.

To the amazement of one and all, including I am damn sure Brain himself, he misses. He tries again and Brain blocks it with his forearm and ankle sweeps him onto his ass. In the same blink of an eye he smashes and elbow into the red head's face and puts a sweet roundhouse kick alongside the Hispanic guy's head. All three of them are now on the floor.

Keela's mouth is wide open in shock. She still tends to think of Brain as a big goofy computer nerd even though she knows he has been training with me and even after seeing him in action last night.

Me, well I am all fucking smiles.

Brain has an advantage these guys don't. They train against an instructor or each other. He trains against me and I have been slowly upping the speed I use with him. So lately he has been training against a faster than human normal target. Also he trains with the laser like focus and dedication he brings to everything that he does. It is what has made him one of the top computer gurus in the world, it is what has made him a multibillionaire and it is what will make him one hell of a Gun someday.

Morton waddles up doing a long slow clap. He stood next to Keela and took in the scene.

"Most impressive my young friend, most impressive indeed. Joseph, I must say that you have done wonders with him in such a short time. After you lose your last mark and should you by chance survive that particular experience, we need to talk to you about working with some of our new Guns. You are apparently one hell of a trainer."

He turned his attention to the three on the floor and they visibly cringed beneath his hard stare.

"Gentlemen, what have we learned?" His tone is dry and scathing and he flicks the words at them like a whip.

"We underestimated him." The biggest one said sullenly.

"Indeed. Get up all of you. You look ridiculous down there. Now, if we are done with the circus sideshow, might you three please follow me to my office?"

As we walk in he activates the usual sound and video recording equipment and then sits wearily behind his desk. He looks like crap, dark circles under his eyes and new lines on his face. This crisis has been hard on all of us.

"Tell me everything."

We do, he is a good officer. He knows when to listen and when to interrupt with meaningful questions. Taking turns we tell him everything that happened, everything that was said and every gut instinct and hunch that we have.

"It pains me more than you could understand to say this, but you are of course correct. We have a leak, a high level one at that. The attack last night was aimed directly at you. I am offering you sanctuary here if you so wish, I will hand pick guards and make your safety my own personal responsibility." He offers.

Screw that.

"Were the bodies from last night identified?" Keela asks him placing her hand on mine.

"Yes, all turned out to be recent missing persons. They were abducted and turned for this specific purpose no doubt. An elder vamp had to have been involved in this, only an elder could have turned and controlled that many newbies. The meeting between the vampire Council and The Order is set for tonight, just after sunset and it will be held here. They have formally requested your presence Joseph, but if you chose to attend I cannot guarantee your safety."

I laugh at that and all three of them turn to look at me like I have grown a third eye or something. I am sorry but for me to beg off because what I need to do isn't safe, is like a deep sea diver complaining that the water is too wet today.

"We aren't really in a safe line of work Morton. I will be there and we decline the protective custody. I would rather be a moving target than a sitting duck."

"And we just plain old don't trust you." Brain tells him cheerfully.

Actually I do, to a degree anyway. Morton is a ruthless little bastard when it comes to serving our Order but I can't see him being in bed with either the vampires or a faction within our Order that wants war. I think the conspiracy has to be a pay grade or two above him which is not good news for us. Also, if Morton decided that my being dead best served our cause, he would have the balls to attempt the job himself.

"On a more positive note our White Adepts think that they have come up with a ritual to gather the Banshee and return them to the realm they came from. They plan on using you as the focus of that ritual Joseph. We plan on sharing that information with the vampire Council tonight. Are you willing to be part of the ritual? It is not without risks I am afraid"

I grit my teeth because I am likely the only Gun he would ask that question of. Morton opposed my induction into The Order vehemently but at the time my mentor Michael Gunn had outranked him. I am all too aware that I am seen as sketchy within the very organization that I have pledged my life to, but such reminders were less than pleasant.

"I serve my Order."

He gives me a long level stare and then a small nod. Coming from him that is like getting a dozen roses and a note of apology.

"Very well, be here tonight at darkfall. Senior members of our Order and a contingent from the vampire Council will meet here, downstairs in the main conference room. The Intervention will provide security on our side and no doubt the Council will bring its own mercenaries and other forms of security. You will testify strictly about the events surrounding our fight against The Morrigan. Senior officers will discuss the ritual that our White Adepts wish to attempt."

His voice holds a tone of dismissal so we all stand up and move towards the door. On the way out I tap him on the shoulder.

"So Morton, during this next ritual if you could not shoot me I would truly appreciate it." I tell him trying desperately not to smile.

During the attempt to seal The Morrigan in her realm Morton had succumbed to powerful waves of violence pouring out of the rift she had been sealed into and snapped. He had been compelled to shoot me and before he could finish the job Keela had smacked him across the back of the head with her gun.

I was just a big enough dick to give him crap about it just about every time I saw him.

He glares at me for a moment but then through the tiredness a rueful smile wins its way through.

"I make no promises." He tells me and turns down a hallway and walks slowly down it.

Fair enough.

The three Guns give us hard stares as we walk by. Brain swaggers by and gives them a little wave.

I sweep his feet under him in one to fast too follow move and set him down just as hard as I can on his ass.

"Don't get cocky trainee." I tell him as I walk by him. Keela stops and helps him up.

The biggest of the Guns gives me the smallest of nods which I return. Most of the Guns do their best to ignore me so it is nice to get a little acknowledgement. In that I hate always being the last kid picked for sports sort of way.

But that is not why I just knocked my friend on his ass. He has done extremely well and come a very long way in a very short time and I respect the effort involved in all that. In a perfect world someone would hand him a shiny prize to validate his pride in his accomplishments.

Our world is violent and unforgiving and getting cocky in ones skills is just a ticket to the graveyard.

Enough things were trying to kill us, no sense in giving them any help.

CHAPTER SIX

As we get close to the car Brain takes out his magic wand and checks the car for bugs and for things that go boom. He takes his time and goes over every square inch and uses a mirror to check the undercarriage. The car comes up clean so we all pile in and take off.

We will find another random dirt bag motel to hole up in until the meeting tonight. A lot is riding on the White Adepts plans, we need to solve the Banshee problem and let us Guns go back to what we do best.

Taking out killer vamps.

I look over at Keela. She's rubbing absently at the small tattoo the Fey tattoo artist Rhune gave her to help protect her from invasive dark magic.

"It itches." She tells me with a small smile.

That's when Brain sees the black van from last night coming up fast on our left.

"Guns out people we have company!" He shouts as he punches the gas to stay ahead of them. A savage grin spills across his face as he changes gears, he loves fast cars and he loves to drive them fast. In another life he would have been an awesome stunt driver in Hollywood. He punches a button on the CD player and the voice of The King of Rock and Roll fills the car.

Well it's one for the money….

"Get us off the damn highway and away from all these civilians!" I bark at him. Keela opens a hidden compartment and takes out two High Point .45 caliber carbines and hands me one. Sometimes shit calls for something heavier than 9mm.

Why a forty five you ask? Because they don't make a forty six.

I slap in a ten round magazine loaded up with what I like to call, a buffet of bad news. A mixed load of hollow points, armor piercing, incendiary and critical defense rounds. Reaching up I open the sun roof, hell the only reason to even have a sunroof in Seattle is to be able to pop up through it and shoot at the bad guys.

And two for the show…

Brain takes an exit and our friends in the van take the bait and follow after us. They are weaving in and out of traffic trying to get ahead of us and cut us off but that ain't gonna happen with my friend at the wheel. He keeps them behind us, he could lose them but that isn't the general idea right now. We need to resolve this quickly and without collateral damage.

Keela is locked and loaded. She sticks two more clips in her pocket and hands me two more. Her hands shake a little from the adrenaline rush but I know that when it comes down to it she will shoot straight.

Three to get ready…

Brain spots a huge mostly deserted Walmart parking lot coming up on our right. He points it out to me and quirks an eyebrow.

"Do it!"

This earns me another savage grin and he twists the wheel hard and roars into the parking lot. The van comes in right behind us and Brain slams on the brakes and spins us around to face them.

And go cat go….

I pop up through the sunroof and Keela opens the front door and takes up position behind it. We both open up at the same moment. Her shots take out the two front tires and she puts the rest in the radiator and engine block of the van.

All ten of mine go right through the front windshield because I wish to send a clear and extremely understandable message to our enemies.

Don't fucking step on my mother fucking blue suede shoes assholes.

An older man stumbles from the van holding a hand to his blood soaked side, he stumbles a few feet and lurches unsteadily into a shadow cast by a parking sign and vanishes.

Dark Adepts. Traveling through shadows is one of their more annoying talents. The Master vampire who had tried to turn me had a human servant who was also a Dark Adept. His name had been Jeremy. He had slammed Keela's head into a wall severely fracturing her skull and then he had stepped into a shadow to escape my response to such behavior.

I then reached into the shadow and pulled his ass back out. He had been quite shocked at my ability to do so, he had been even more shocked when I tore his heart out and showed it to him before he died.

One of Brain's countless theories is that since the aborted dark ritual that was supposed to transform me into a magic wielding vampire, I probably now have the ability to travel through shadows just like the Dark Adepts do. Haven't tested that theory for a number of reasons.

First reason, being that which I am, I have more than enough stain on my soul without dabbling in dark magic.

Second reason, I have fuck all idea of how that would work. Don't relish the idea of being lost in the shadows forever or ending up in a room full of pissed off Dark Adepts who don't want to play nice with me.

We ditch the carbines and draw our hand guns and all three of us carefully walk up on the van. There are two more people in the van both very dead. There are also a box of hand grenades and a couple of guns on the floor by the passenger side. The van reeks of dark magic.

I want to test a theory of my own that I have, so I grab the smaller of the two bodies and carry it over to the shadow his buddy disappeared into. I toss him in and watch carefully.

The body lies there for about two seconds and then vanishes.

Brain and I exchange a look and without any words being said we come up with a nasty idea. Keela stands by looking out for more trouble as we pick up the last body and carry it over to the shadows.

Brain pulls the pin on a grenade and stuffs it in the asshole's jacket pocket. We then toss him into the shadow where he too disappears.

We trade high fives, whoever and whatever is on the end of that particular underground rail road is due for an unpleasant surprise.

"We need to get the hell out of here Joe." Brain says gesturing towards the slack jawed crowd that is beginning to form a safe distance away from us. As is the case more often than not lately, we are the cause of the sirens we can already hear approaching.

"I'll drive brother. You send Morton an update about what fun we have had this morning since leaving him."

On the way back to the car I pull Keela to me and give her a quick hug and kiss.

"And you, if that scar every itches again you let us know."

Back into the car and back on the road. We stop at the first used car lot we come across and make the salesman's day by swapping Brain's nice car for one worth a lot less. He doesn't question why we want to make such an obviously bad deal and we don't offer the information. The guy can't get us out the door fast enough. It is all over in the time it takes to sign a few papers.

We transfer all of our gear hidden and otherwise to the new car, a nondescript brown and boring as hell 2000 Ford Taurus with lightly tinted windows. Brain sighs as he starts it up. It probably offends his mega car buffs sensibilities to drive such a mundane vehicle. He has great and very expensive taste in his cars but, serving The Order means such occasional sacrifices.

"Cheer up brother! At least we didn't total one of your cars this time." I tell him as I slap him on the back.

Oddly he seems to take no comfort from that.

"We don't total my cars Joe. You total my cars, just you. There is no we involved in totaling my cars. It is you and you alone who does that." He reminds me uncharitably.

Keela stifles a giggle, she has been along for the ride before when bad things have happened to his cars. Like the time we crashed into a pissed off vampire at eighty plus miles an hour. Like anyone plans on doing that, so not my fault.

Whatever….

Time to get off everyone's radar until tonight's sit down with the vampire council. Killing our pursuers and swapping out cars ought to buy us enough time to find some food and another no tell motel, where cash will buy us a nice anonymous room.

I look over at Keela and take a long moment to enjoy the way that the Flogging Molly t-shirt that she stole from Brain after 'accidently' shrinking it in the laundry fits her curves.

She catches me looking and gives me a quick and heated smile in return that rattles my cage like it always does.

Yeah, new plan.

We will make that two rooms.

CHAPTER SEVEN

We pull into the warehouse's parking lot just as the sun is setting. Already there are several luxury SUV's with darkly tinted windows parked close to the entrance. Their doors open and the elders of the vampire Council and their entourage of lesser vamps and human servants step out. They brought no Renfields of course, not creating blood slaves is one of the laws that The Order imposes on the vampire world. It is punishable, as are most of our laws, by death.

I can feel the elders from here, like a hot weight settling down on me. My marks burn and I have to take a deep breath and push all of the sensations to a locked box in the back of my mind so they don't distract me from the business at hand.

The night hums with vampire energies, I glance at Keela and Brain and I wonder how it can be that they can't feel them. A squad of vampire hired mercenaries' spills out of two of the SUV's and they fan out surrounding the building. I can't see them but I know that The Intervention has already surrounded them.

A dozen or so vamps, all over two hundred years old, also position themselves around the building in a loose circle. Extra muscle to deal with whatever might come of this night. I sincerely hope that the vampires came to talk because if they didn't, well, we kill some of them but they will kill all of us.

Such a move of course would lead to their own destruction. Even if they wiped us out to the last Gun, The Order would send in troops from other cities to wipe out the Council and all offending vampires down to the last one.

Not sure how it works across the pond but in this country the vampires have divided the territory up into five districts. Each district has its own ruling Council and each district has its own capital city.

Lucky us, Seattle is the capital of our lovely district.

Our Order is therefore divided up in much the same way. I have been sent occasionally to other districts to help out during major bouts of trouble and I have also occasionally worked with Guns from other districts who have come here to help. No doubt there are a few such here in the city now with all that is going on here.

The vampire Council is in the building now as no doubt are the senior officers of The Order. The rest of us rabble will wait out here until we are summoned.

Janelle appears in front of me out of nowhere, speak of the devil and up pops a reasonable facsimile thereof.

"The Council would hear your words now, Black Irish." She tells me and then vanishes back into the night.

It is show time. With Brain on one side of me and my girl Keela on the other, we walk in to find out what the night has in store for us. Normally we wouldn't bring weapons into the warehouse but tonight is an exception, everyone will be armed.

The meeting room has been set up with a long table on each side, one for the vampire Council and one for the senior officers of my Order. A Gun stands behind each officer with his gun out but pointed down at the floor. Each vampire elder has an attendant standing behind them as well. In each corner of the room stands a White Adept casting spells of protection.

The head of the vampire council stands up as I come into the room, the sheer weight of her years hits me like a fist and I have to steel myself not to flinch before her. She is the single oldest vampire I have ever encountered, older even than our new pal, Avanticus who sits to her left with Janelle standing behind him.

She has to be almost two thousand years old and power simply boils around her in an almost visible aura. Almost like watching heat ripple up from hot asphalt on a blistering hot summer day. She is almost seven feet tall and unlike most ancients she still has fine white hair cut very short covering her head, looking almost like feathers.

Her power seethes around me and I have to fight the impulse to kneel before her. She calls to the vampire taint inside of me and it is eager to respond, the Banshee part of me also responds and that is perhaps what allows me to remain standing. She is so powerful she has come close to rolling me under her will without even looking at me.

Then she looks at me.

Her bottomless eyes pin me to the spot that I am standing in. They bore relentlessly into me, taking my measure, turning me inside out and shaking any secrets I thought I might be keeping out. I can only stand here and hope that she will eventually allow me to breathe.

"You may call me Ennod. Come before us then, Black Irish. Come before us and speak only the truth to me and mine." It is both invitation and command.

Her power recedes enough for me to do a few simple things, breathe, move think, stuff like that. So I walk out into the middle of the room and face a panel of ancient vampires, any and all of which could squash me like a bug.

I took public speaking way back in the day, in high school and it in no way prepared me for something like this. Just another way that public education has failed me.

Taking in a deep breathe I lay it all out for them. All of the events leading up to the Banshee escaping into our world and the way that I kept their queen mother from joining them. I also tell them all that has happened since, Avanticus approached us. It is a little like talking to an oil painting, no one moves. Nobody even blinks or breathes they all just stare at me as I talk. I can sense Ennod weighing and tasting each word that I speak for the truth. It makes me want to be extremely truthful.

"Lies! All lies! You deliberately released this plague upon us Black Irish! I can only imagine that you meant to bring The Morrigan amongst us as well but that part of the plan failed somehow, thank the darkness!" A tall black elder stands up and shouts at me.

"Silence, Bernard. Do you think so little of my power that you think this human, different from the rest as he is, can stand before me and tell me lies? Sit down and mind your fool tongue." Ennod tells him in a bored tone.

Bernie doesn't like it much but he sits back down still obviously fuming. A buzz of muttered conversation goes through the council too low for me to make out words. It ends abruptly as she raises a pale hand.

"A moment to take care of other business now, I would have the name of the vampire who ordered the attack on this human and his companions last night. It was agreed amongst us that no actions were to be taken until I deemed fit. Today's attack by Dark Adepts I can dismiss for there is no proof of vampire involvement but someone here arranged the fledgling vampire attack. I would have their name." Her voice is crisp and resonates with power.

Nobody steps up to claim credit. She cast her eyes over her people looking at them one by one but nobody broke under the weight of that gaze.

Tough fucking crowd.

"Very well then, I will make my own investigation and darkness help the vampires responsible. Moving on, tell us of this solution you have spoken of."

Morton stands up and bows deeply to the Council table, apparently he will be speaking tonight even though I see at least two officers that outrank him. Probably because he knows the most about whatever ritual it is that the White Adepts wish to attempt. The Order is not as rank sensitive as other organizations, talent and knowledge often trump rank.

"Our White Adepts think that by using Joseph as a focus they can do a very complex drumming ritual that should call all of the Banshee in the city to him. He will be the focus of the spell, once they are gathered they will be lulled asleep and then using Joseph's connection with the rift, we will open it briefly and return them to slumber with their queen mother." He tells them.

There is calm confidence in his voice that I doubt very much that he actually feels.

"Forgive me, are you saying that we are taking the risk of opening the rift between worlds and waking The Morrigan up again?" Avanticus asks calmly.

"The rift would be open for seconds and then resealed. I will not lie and say there is no risk but our Adepts are confident it can be done."

"Madness! Are we gullible children to be swayed by calm words? They wish to…" Whatever Bernie was going to say he never got a chance to finish.

In a blur of movement far too fast for even my eyes to follow Ennod rushed to his end of the table, tore his head off and sat back down with the head in front of her. Blood leaking from the head, staining the tablecloth and dripping slowly down onto the floor.

His headless body falls from the chair he had been sitting in and lies twitching on the floor.

Clean up on aisle five.

"He was beginning to vex me." She told the room at large in a flat tone.

Note to self, don't go vexing Ennod.

It seems like a poor life choice.

"The plan obviously has its risks, but then so does inaction. I find it hard to believe that your Order which has so long been pledged to protecting human life would do something deliberately that would cause the violent deaths of untold numbers." She tells Morton in measured tones.

From outside the building comes the sound of heavy weapons fire and the very faint sound of Banshee screeching. Some of the younger vamps standing behind the council table cover their ears and flinch.

"Please everyone remain seated! Let the forces outside deal with whatever the situation is." Morton holds up his hand as he calls for calm.

Several long tense minutes pass before two messengers come into the room, one goes straight to Ennod and whispers urgently in her ear and the other goes straight to Morton and does the same.

"Well then, it would appear that our combined forces working together just turned aside a major Banshee assault on this building. We shall take such cooperation as a good omen for this solution you wish to attempt. You may proceed with your plans." She tells us in a formal tone.

Hate to tell her but we weren't actually asking for permission.

She claps her hands once sharply and the room is simply empty of vampires. A few human servants trail out behind them looking a little embarrassed by their lack of speed.

Morton walks up to me with an officer I don't recognize trailed by two beefy Guns. Keela and Brain come and stand behind me.

"Joseph this is the officer in charge, Lawrence. Lawrence this is Joseph Gunn, his trainee Brian and a Widow in service to us by the name of Keela." He makes the introductions.

He is a stuffy looking prick, grey hair in a severe military buzz cut and the kind of posture you get only by having a stick up your ass. He is almost as tall as I am but he is carrying a lot more weight on his frame than I am and none of it is muscle.

"How's it hanging Larry?" I ask as I offer him my hand.

Yeah, not really big on the whole saluting thing.

After a moment's hesitation he takes it but I think that after the handshake he will be plunging his hand into a vat of hand sanitizer. I get the strong ass feeling that we aren't going to be big buddies.

I hate it how right I am sometimes.

"Joseph Gunn you will accompany these men to a detention cell. Your friends will be held in separate cells."

Keela, Brain and I draw our guns just as the muscle standing behind Larry does the same. If this thing goes south it is going to get loud and messy up in here.

"Enough! Stand down all of you at once. Lawrence don't be a horse's ass. Joseph you are crucial to the rituals that the Adepts wish to attempt, give me your word that you will not leave the building tonight. We simply cannot risk anything happening to you." Morton wades in and stands between all of us.

"Despite what you, or anyone else for that matter thinks of me Morton, I serve my Order." I hiss at him through clenched teeth.

Morton looks sad and suddenly old as he waves the two muscle bound Guns away. Behind him Larry blusters and fumes.

"And despite what you think of me Joseph, I have never doubted it. Please make use of the main apartment upstairs. I will provide guards not to imprison you but to keep you safe." He says softly.

"This is outrageous Morton! I will have you stripped of your rank!" Larry steps towards the smaller man.

He doesn't make it.

Keela whips out a knife in one smooth move, has it next to the idiot's throat, pressing just hard enough not to draw blood.

Oops, I mean almost hard enough not to draw blood. A thin trickle is running down his neck.

"Look at it this way Larry, if the ritual works you will be free to file complaint form A with the proper authorities and they might even read it someday. If it doesn't and all-out war breaks out, well, then we are likely all dead and it won't matter much. What you need to decide right now is if you want to get a head start on the whole being dead and things not mattering part." She tells him in a bright perky voice.

God, I love that girl.

He turns bright red and a vein in his forehead is doing a mamba beat, maybe he will stroke out and save us all some trouble.

No such luck but he does back away slowly and then turn on his heel and stomps away.

For right now we will call that a win.

Morton lets out a low chuckle and slaps a manila folder into my hands before he waddles away.

"Notes on tomorrow's ritual Joseph please be so kind as to study them." He calls back over his shoulder.

He points at a couple of guards and gestures towards us and they walk over to stand by us. They don't look happy with the assignment but they will follow their field officer's order.

With friends like mine who the hell needs guards anyway?

Keela puts the knife away and leads the way and we all troop up the industrial steel stairs to the upper levels of the warehouse, our guards trailing discretely behind us.

The apartment will have a kitchen, the kitchen will have a fridge and God willing the fridge will have beer.

CHAPTER EIGHT

The apartment is richly decorated in early American whatever the hell is lying around. A couple of battered couches, a cigarette burn scarred coffee table and mismatched every damn thing. A poster of Bella Lugosi hangs on one wall because somebody thought it would be funny.

Well, yeah it kind of is.

I check the fridge and there is beer, more proof, if any was needed that God doesn't actually hate me.

Brain holds a finger to his lips and starts scanning the entire place with that wand of his. He looks in places that would never occur to me. He is quick and very thorough and he finds several bugs. He shows me the video display and six little red dots show up.

He pushes a tiny button on his ungodly expensive wristwatch and suddenly all the little red dots vanish.

"Ok James Bond what did you do?" Keela asks him in a teasing tone as she curls up on one end of the couch.

"Narrowly broadcast modified electromagnetic pulse." He tells her with a casual shrug.

A guy and his gadgets, I swear he is like a walking talking Swiss Army Knife sometimes.

I hand each of them a cold beer and sit down next to my girl. I am still riding the high of her getting in the face of our pal Larry.

"Girl, tell us the truth now, would you really have cut that moron?" I ask her laughing.

She blushes at first, hell she is an ex nun after all. But then she looks me in the eyes and tells me.

"Not sure, good thing we didn't have to go through all the mess of finding out."

"Girl, I have been a bad influence on you."

"Yes, you have." She flashes me a wicked smile that makes me fervently wish that this apartment had more than one bedroom and the Brain had somewhere else to be.

There is a knock at the door and Brain stands up with his gun in his hand to answer it.

"Yo, trainee. Want to come spar?" The red headed Gun who Brain took down earlier pokes his head in the door.

The Lord works in mysterious ways.

He looks over at me his eyes asking for permission, I nod at him to go at the same time I shoot the other Gun a stern look spelling out that I want my trainee back in more or less the same shape I am sending him out in.

The Gun flashes me a grin that says, yeah we might make him hurt but we won't really hurt him.

They leave and Keela and I sit on the couch together staring at each other. I take a moment to take her in, this unlikely love of mine. The fact that we found each other despite all the odds against it has reformed my relationship with the God I once thought hated me.

Lesson learned, God hates no one.

That being said all of our choices and behaviors have consequences and I am living this life to pay the consequences of mine.

I smile at my girl and lean in for a kiss.

She smiles back at me for a moment but then gets a queasy and alarmed look on her face. She stands up and rushes back to the small bathroom where I can hear her being nosily and violently sick.

Not knowing what the fuck is going on or what to do to help, I do the guy thing and sit there with a, what the hell is going on look on my face.

I am pretty good at it.

After a few minutes I hear her splashing water on her face and she comes back and sits next to me. Nothing happens for a couple of minutes, we just sit there. She reaches over and takes my hand in hers and gives it a hard squeeze.

"I'm pregnant."

I burst out laughing and she bursts into tears at the exact same moment and I tell you that, with a damn gun to my head, I would not be able to tell you which of us responded most appropriately.

Brain comes back a while later, he is limping slightly but otherwise seems none the worse for wear from his sparring session. He comes in and helps himself to a beer from the fridge and plops himself down on the couch, across from the one Keela and I are snuggled up against each other on.

"What's up guys?" He asks and then he opens his bottle of beer and takes a long pull off of it.

"We are having a baby." We tell him in unison.

He will never believe us in a thousand years but our intention was absolutely not to have him inhale beer and then spray it out of his nose.

That was more of a bonus really.

After he recovers and he has offered us his congratulations, I hand him the file that Morton gave me and tell him to go through it. Part of his training has been reading ritual and simple magic. He is actually a tad better at basic spells like masking spells than I am, for the simple reason that he is completely human. With my vampire taint I shouldn't even be able to wield any magic but then again I am the glaring exception to a lot of rules like that.

After he looks it over he frowns and gives me a long look. I know what he is going to tell me before he says it.

"You can tell me that I'm wrong Joe, hell you taught me how to read this stuff yourself but it seems a little long on maybes, what ifs and good intentions."

He isn't wrong, it is far from the most concrete ritual I have ever seen mapped out. I am sure that The Order has rushed the White Adepts into a, Hail Mary we really hope this works approach, because they needed something to tell the vampire Council. A lot will depend on the skill of the Adepts involved and I know that Morton will hand select the best available ones.

Keela is on the other side of the room putzing around in the kitchen, Brain leans forward and lowers his voice.

"I want you to know Joe that if anything were to happen to you I would take care of Keela and the baby." He tells me solemnly.

I look at him fondly, this friend that against all odds, life has served up to me. He hadn't had to tell me that for me to know that it was true, but it was nice to hear it out loud.

"Thank you brother."

The baby is a game changer, it is if you are a civilian or a vampire hunter or at least it should be. Time to reconsider this life, if the ritual succeeds I will go back to paying my penance until the last mark is gone. If I survive that, I will take Morton up on his offer to become a trainer. I will still be serving the cause but each day won't be a, will or won't I die today, crap shoot. We will settle into a new life, not white picket fences mind you but a hell of a lot closer to it than the life we live now.

As of right now Keela herself is out of the game. If we had known she was pregnant when we were attacked, both Brain and I would have been distracted by the overwhelming need to protect her. That distraction could have gotten any and all of us killed. The Order will just have to make do with one less Widow for a while.

The sad fact is that new ones are being created all the time.

I look at Brain and wonder if it is over between him and Jenny, he hasn't said much about it but we have been pretty busy trying to stay alive. She has been good for him in a lot of ways, he is as happy as I have seen him since vampires killed his wife years ago and he entered this life. If they are going to be together she has a lot to adapt to. For his own sake I hope that she can, but in the life of a Gun such happiness as Keela and I share is very rare. I wish it for my friend but he has long odds to beat.

Tomorrow we will attempt the ritual, attempt to restore the balance, precarious that it is, that has always existed between the world of the vampires and our own.

But for now I will sit on a lumpy couch and have a beer with my best friend and watch the soon to be mother of my child pretend she knows how to cook. I don't know what she is making but the smell is not promising.

No matter what it ends up tasting like, I will eat it with a smile because I know that it was prepared with love.

I am getting so damn smart in my old age.

CHAPTER NINE

Morning comes with a knock at the door. Brain answers it with his big ass pistol in his hand. He lets Morton and the psychic, the one who helped close the door in my mind that connected me to The Morrigan, in. Her name is Josephine and she is in a White Adepts robe.

She takes one look at Keela and lets out a happy squeal and moves quickly over to her to give her a hug.

"Congratulations!" She beams at me.

Hard keeping secrets from a psychic.

They kind of suck that way.

Morton stands there looking a little baffled and Brain takes pity on him and fills him in.

"She is with child." He tells him gravely.

A look I can't decipher flashes so quickly across his face that I am half sure I imagined it. Whatever it was is gone as he shakes my hand and offers me his congratulations.

"This is new." I tell Josephine gesturing at the white robe. Last time I saw her she was Morton's go to psychic but I had no idea she was also a White Adept.

"It has long been a goal of mine to study the mysteries Joseph. I earned my robe just last summer." Her smile is modest but I can hear the pride in her voice.

"She has risen quickly in her coven and will be leading today's ritual." Morton says with pride in his own voice.

Something clicks in my head and I look at the two of them standing close to one another, the spaces between them overlapping somehow the way it is with some couples.

Well fuck me gently with a chainsaw.

"Yes Joseph, we are together, have been for some time now. What of it?" Josephine asks me in a challenging tone.

"Everyone in the room who knew that these two were bumping uglies raise your hand." I demand incredulously.

Keela puts her hand straight up and after a couple of seconds Brain sheepishly raises his as well.

Screw all the nice things I said about the guy being my best friend, he is obviously an asshole for not telling me.

"Fine, I am an unobservant idiot, can we move on to what we will be doing today?" I sound petulant even to myself.

"What is going to happen will come in two stages, we already have a sacred drum circle set up. They will build a rhythm using Bodhran and other types of drums that the White Adepts will infuse with their own magic. You will act as both focus of the spell and a lure to call the Banshee to you. Once you have collected them the nature of the drumming and magic will change and hopefully put the Banshee into the same manner of sleep as their queen mother." Morton tells me trying very hard to sound confident.

"And then Joseph, I will use both my psychic gifts and my magic to open the door in your mind between you and the realm of the Banshee. We will then send the Banshee through and reclose the door." Josephine says in her soft voice.

"And then it's Miller time." Brain quips.

Morton looks at him like he is a disgusting mess on the bottom of his shoes and Brain withers just a little under his stare.

Hell, I thought it was funny.

"All of this has never been attempted before, Joseph. Magic, like all things is continuously evolving and now it must evolve to meet this new threat."

Josephine says laying her hand on my arm. As always she carries with her the subtle hint of jasmine.

"The Intervention will of course provide security. Ms. Keela I am afraid that I will have to insist that you remain behind, due to your...delicate condition. It simply will not be safe to expose an unborn baby to the sheer amount of powers that we will be manipulating." Morton tells her sternly in a tone that invites no debate.

She hesitates but then gives him a tiny nod.

"Bring him back to me." She tells him.

"My word as an officer of The Order that I will do all that is possible to make that happen." He tells her gravely with a small bow.

"Brian, you will stand by your mentors side and watch his back. While he is emerged in the magic he will not be able to defend himself. That task will by necessity fall to you."

"I serve The Order." Brain uses the ritual reply that I have taught him, holding his right fist clenched over his heart.

"Very soon now Joseph, we will have to talk about inducting your young friend here. Despite a certain callow immaturity he may at some point not embarrass you as full Gun. That is more of a testament to your training than any inherent talent he may have." Morton tells me with a slightly amused quirk of an eyebrow. Nobody does eyebrow quirks like our pal Morty.

Well, maybe Spock.

"Much remains to be done so I will take my leave of you now." Morton bows to the room in general and walks out of the apartment.

Josephine watches him go with a fond and slightly sad smile. Now that I know what to look for I can see how much she cares for him.

No accounting for taste.

At once that seems unkind to me and I glance over at Keela, I imagine there are those that might say the same of us.

Jeez, tell a guy he is about to be a father and he starts showing signs of empathy and emotional maturity.

I am really much, much better at sarcasm.

"Take this Joseph and have your lady love anoint every inch of your body with this sacred oil." She instructs me handing me a small cobalt blue glass bottle.

She places a soft finger against my lips before I can make the obvious comment about inches and shakes her head gently at me.

"This is not the time for jokes Joseph Gunn. If you fail to take this seriously I will task your protégé with this particular task."

"Wow, look at the time will ya? I had better go arrange a security detail for Keela for while we are gone."

Brain is out the door so fast it almost seems like he carries the vampire taint instead of me.

Josephine shakes a finger the color of coffee with a little milk in it at me and then she too leaves.

I look at my girl holding the jar of oil. I think about being alone with my girl with a jar of oil that she is supposed to anoint "Every inch of my body with."

All things considered I have had plenty of days that started out worse than this.

CHAPTER TEN

We pull up to the site of the rift, right next to the Fremont troll of all places. All ready things are going better than last time for the simple reason that no one fired a rocket launcher at us as we arrived.

The drummers are already in place, if you are thinking about the drum circles, bored, stoned suburban kids do at places like Hempfest, think again. Each of these drummers is a full-fledged Shamanistic practitioner. That being said, I can smell the pungent aroma of high quality marijuana in the air, everyone has their own path to touching power.

It was hard leaving Keela behind but this is no place for her now. We said our brave goodbyes like the soldiers that we both are. Doesn't mean it hurts any less, just means that we know our duty.

The drummers surround a ring of White Adepts holding hands in a ring around Josephine who stands alone in the very center of that ring.

The Church doesn't officially acknowledge the existence of either white or dark magic. That doesn't change the fact that I can already feel the first subtle stirrings of white magic building in the very air around us, radiating up from the earth we stand on.

A small distance away are parked three black limousines. A contingent of human servants representing their vampire masters in this day's work. I flick my senses at them, all are strong human servants but none are Dark Adepts. They will keep a watchful eye on what we are doing and at nightfall when their various masters rise they will give full reports. Some of them are armed but that is only to be expected, the world is after all a very dangerous place.

As I walk up to Josephine she smiles and I can feel it in my mind. She holds out both hands in invitation as Brain and I enter the circle. She gestures slightly and I feel the circle reclose behind us. Brain goes into bodyguard alert mode and stands behind me and slightly to my left. He is busy trying to look in all directions at once.

She regards him and his drawn weapon with disapproval but she knows enough to know that it is necessary. She turns her back on him and faces me, her eyes already shining with power.

The drums begin a complex rhythm and the Adepts begin a low chant that beats in a counter rhythm. Magic surrounds and pulls at all the various things inside of me. It pulls the hardest at the Banshee in me and it pulls the least strongly at my vampire taint because it is a thing of death and the powers being formed here now are attuned to the forces of life.

"Hail *Fennid,* Hail *Rifennid.* Hail Joseph Gunn." Josephine intones formally as she takes my hands in hers. When we touch the magic flowing around us pulses strongly and then returns to the rhythms it is being set to.

"You are the focus and anchor of this spell, do you accept that role?" Her voice echoes with power.

"I do." My own voice holds the first stirring of energies now.

"Then let it begin." She says simply and closes her eyes.

The drumming becomes louder now and even more impossibly complex. It blocks out every other sensation until only it remains. It blocks out all conscious thought. The universe narrows down to this point, to only the magic seething and boiling all around us. The magic waiting to be given shape and purpose. The Adepts blend their power seamlessly into the magic of the drummers and I can feel Josephine straining to both control and augment that power. I can feel her in my mind and I feel the essence of her interwoven into the magic pulsing around us.

The energies build to a crescendo, as they do the ritual begins to give those energies shape purpose and direction.

Go forth then and seek…

The magic flows through me using me as a divining rod of sorts. It sniffs at that which is Banshee in me, like a tracking dog getting the scent before being sent out on the hunt. I feel it as it catches that scent.

And then the spell ripples out in one sharply defined massive wave through the entire city. It fills the city like water fills a cup and it finds and touches each and every Banshee spirit contained within its borders. To each of them the spell begins to whisper softly and tug at them.

Come to us, come home...

The rhythm increases its pace and the invitation moves to a suggestion and then to a command. One by one the Banshee spirits are drawn out of their human hosts, they struggle but the magic pulls at them exhausting them until their resistance is done and they succumb to the power ensnaring them. They are drawn out kicking and screaming but they are drawn out all the same.

I am the focus, I am the draw. They are being pulled towards me. I can feel them out there, each individual spasm of resistance and I do what it is that I was brought here for.

I open my mouth and I add my own song to the flow of power.

I can feel Josephine smile in approval in my mind as the low atonal sound blends in flawlessly to the spell unfolding all around us. The drummers and the Adepts take the new power being offered and add it to their efforts.

The addition of my power turns the tide and we begin to gain the upper hand.

To the Banshee spirits now I am the magnet and they are the steel filings, they are drawn despite all resistance to me. Slowly, ever so slowly but faster and faster now they begin to come to me. Coming from all parts of the city, some near some farther away but all of them are coming to me.

I am lost in the magic now, there is no crisis, there are no doubts, there exist no worry or fear. The magic is part of me and I am part of the magic. I am lost in the power and raw beauty of the spell.

Come to us now...

They begin to appear before us now, a few at first and then more and more. Brightly burning red sparks glittering before me. I can see them before me even though my eyes are closed, I can feel them resisting me but being drawn here none the less.

A new note is being woven into the spell now, I can feel it. A subtle sub rhythm in both the drumming and the chanting wrapping itself around the song that I am singing into the magic. It is a soothing, lulling tone that speaks of well-deserved rest. It washes out over the gathered Banshee spirits and slowly I sense their angry red light fading, fading away first to a sullen crimson glow.

Come to us now and rest...

They are all here, now, before me gathered it would seem just out of reach. One by one I watch in my mind's eye as each spark fades and dims away to almost darkness. I sense them succumbing tiny bits at a time to the spell swirling all around us, I sense them quieting by tiny degrees until at last the very last of them go near dark and still.

Once again the spell changes meter and pace and I feel Josephine in my mind telling me what to do next or rather showing me. Her calm presence keeps me centered and on task even as I feel her straining to touch the very outer limits of her own skills and powers.

I open myself up, drop all of my shields and begin to take the quieted Banshee into me. One by one I absorb them into a place deep inside of my being. It seems to go on forever, the magic holding us in this place in this time for this purpose. Josephine smiles in exaltation as the last Banshee spirit is contained inside of me.

She let's go of my hands and raises her own above her head for just a moment and then slashes them both downward.

Then abruptly the drumming and chanting ceases between one beat and the next. The silence seems louder than the drumming somehow.

This portion of the spell is over.

I fall to my knees and after a moment Josephine helps me to struggle to my feet. I note with pride that

Brain resisted the urge to help me and remained on guard. He nods at me and goes back to doing a slow careful scan of our surroundings.

"Well done Joseph." She smiles at me. Excitement and exhaustion seem to be battling it out in her eyes, but excitement seems to be winning.

As I stand up I glance over at the vampire Councils group of observers standing by their limos and wonder what they saw during the ritual. Magic isn't always a very good show, power is often invisible, more perceived than seen. They don't need to be impressed by the show, I suppose, as long as we deliver the expected results. Hoped like Hell that we could oblige.

I can feel the sleeping Banshee spirits inside of me, not individually as when I was absorbing them but collectively. I feel them as a heavy weight in my mind that I long to put down but will carry as long as need be.

"I will now use my psychic gifts to open the door in your mind Joseph, you must work with me to do so. Once open I will show you how to guide the Banshee through that door into the rift and then we seal the rift forever." Josephine tells me quietly touching my arm.

That's when the gunfire starts.

CHAPTER ELEVEN

Cursing Brain shoves me to the ground and crouches over me. He slips me his backup piece and I click the safety off. Fully automatic weapons fire and screams fill the air.

I watch him move towards Josephine knowing he will be too late, her body twitches as multiple bullets slam into it. She goes down and she is dead before she hits the ground.

I feel her die in my mind.

Her wide open dead eyes stare sightlessly at me.

The shooters are targeting the White Adepts and drummers and they are dying all around us. Some are trying to run but they don't get far before they too are mowed down. The scene is bloody pandemonium, sheer carnage. The human servants and body guards are already in their black limos getting the hell out of Dodge, as fast as they can.

Brain is returning fire and moving us toward the car, my head is still reeling from the magic so it takes me a few seconds to figure it out and when I do I stop moving in pure shock.

"God help us." I whisper.

He is tugging at me trying to drag me along with him as he fires in the direction the shots are coming from trying to cover us while we get away.

"Damn it Joe, move for fucks sake!" He yells.

"It's The Intervention. They are killing the Adepts and drummers."

He sucks in his breath as the words hit him. This is betrayal beyond imagining, beyond reason. The elite military force of The Order is slaughtering their own people in broad daylight.

If they wanted us dead right now we would be dead, for some reason some unknown agenda they are letting us get away.

Then Keela pops into my mind and none of this shit matters. All that matters is getting to her and making sure she is safe. I move toward the car at a dead run and Brain fires the last of his rounds and is right behind me.

He drives and we are down the road and away from the awful scene in seconds, leaving God knows how many dead behind us. Josephine's dead face flashes into my mind bringing with it the faint hint of jasmine and a tear rolls down my cheek and I wipe it away angrily, this is no fucking time for tears.

It is time for some motherfucker's head on a stick.

"Fuck! Fuck! Fuck!" Brain screams suddenly pounding his fist on the steering wheel as we careen down the road.

I take a deep breath and center myself. He is a trainee but I am a fully trained Gun. It is time to start acting like one and take control of the situation.

"Dial it down trainee, first order of business is to get to Keela and make sure she is ok." I tell him putting strength into my voice I don't really feel just now.

"And the second order of business?" He asks me making an obviously Herculean effort to calm himself.

"Finding out who or what is behind this and killing them. Now shut the hell up and drive, I need to think." I snap the order at him.

It works, given a task and a direct order helps to center him and he nods at me and turns his attention grimly back to the road.

I slumped into my seat and closed my eyes, falling back into my training to try and calm myself enough to use logical thinking. I did the mental equivalent of dumping a jigsaw puzzle on the floor to look at the pieces and tried to make some semblance of sense out of them.

Someone high up enough in The Order, for their word to be absolute law with The Intervention, had ordered them to kill off the drummers and Adepts.

That much was clear. But why? What was to be gained from it?

It had to be about the timing.

They had allowed the first part of the ritual to be concluded, they had allowed us to contain the Banshee within me. They had only turned on us after that. What could be gained? I couldn't contain the Banshee spirits indefinately, at least I didn't think that I could. Already I had felt slight stirrings from them especially during the slaughter for it had surely called to them. Without Josephine to help me maintain the magic they would eventually free themselves, probably by tearing me to pieces on the way out.

Was that the point? Far easier and less esoteric ways to kill me if that was the goal. No, a bigger game was being played here. I spun it round and round and came to the same conclusion each time.

Did players on either The Council or The Order or both simply want the ritual to fail so that the war they hungered for would come? That didn't seem to fit, they could have stopped the ritual at any time, why let it half succeed?

Once again, it came down to the timing.

They had stopped us before we sent the Banshee back to their realm, therefore someone wanted them for something.

No idea for what but the logic of that made sense to me. I shared my thoughts with Brain as we drove and I could all but see the wheels turning in that fine mind of his.

"Who?" Was all he had asked.

Hell, that was the sixty four thousand dollar question now wasn't it?

We needed to get to Morton somehow, poor bastard's girlfriend was lying on the ground torn apart by bullets, from the very people he had charged with her safety, but I knew him. I knew he would be putting his grief aside and doing what needed to be done. Whoever did this was far above him in rank as I suspected. He would be forming his own suspicions right about now.

The Intervention could have killed me at any moment but that simply would have set the Banshee free again. Or failing that, they could have easily captured me. Whoever wanted the Banshee was using me for the time being as a container of sorts for them. Which means I was allowed to escape because they were confident they could collect me later.

Really didn't like the damn roads that particular thought led me down very much at all.

We need answers, but first we needed to get Keela some place safe. Then and only then would Brain and I be free to go do what needed to be done.

Beat the fucking answers out of somebody.

As many damn somebodies as necessary.

We come squealing around the corner and Brain slams on the brakes and we both just stare for a moment at the scene in front of us.

The warehouse is fully engulfed in flames and several fire trucks are busy spraying water on it trying to contain the blaze. Thick black smoke billows up into the sky and it is obvious that nothing alive could possibly be inside of that inferno.

A sick weary hopeless feeling hits me in a dark wave, it threatens to pull me under. The Banshee writhe in me for a split second responding to it and then go back to their slumbers.

Brain's cellphone rings and after a few rings he answers it numbly. He listens for a few seconds and then hands it to me.

"Even trade Black Irish, your life for hers and that of your unborn child's. Stay tuned for instructions." An electronically garbled voice tells me and then the line goes dead.

Somebody somewhere wants to play Let's Make a Deal.

Somebody somewhere is going to find out just how much I fucking hate games.

CHAPTER TWELVE

Await instructions, the voice on the phone had said. Needing to find a place to do that Brain drove us to the first place that had popped into his head.

We went to Jenny's bar.

She took one look at us when we came in and without a word pointed to the private banquet room off to the left of the main bar area. We went and a few minutes later she stepped in with a bottle of Jamison's whiskey and three glasses.

"You both look like Hell, what happened?" She asks putting the bottle down in front of us.

Brain tells her, his voice is detached almost clinical. He spares no details and as he tells the tale I watch the color drain from her face.

At least she doesn't pull the usual civilian crap of telling us to call the police or FBI or any other damn set of initials. She knows enough about our world to know that isn't one of our options. Instead she pours us each a measure of good Irish whiskey.

"I'm sorry Joe." She says softly.

We aren't here for sympathy, I nod at Brain he gets up and whispers in her ear. He is asking her for the key to the storage locker she has been letting us keep downstairs. If she had any idea of all the things we have in there she would be horrified but so far she has been more or less content with a sort of don't ask don't tell policy.

She has that same policy for much of what we do.

He takes the key and heads off leaving her standing there with a glass of whiskey staring at me.

"What are you going to do?" She asks me finally, maybe only to break the silence.

"I am going to drink this glass of whiskey." I tell her gruffly.

"Not really what I meant." She tells me with a bit of an edge to her voice now.

"Next, I wait for further instructions and then I go play Let's Make a Deal with whoever these assholes happen to be."

She finishes her whiskey and refills both of our glasses from the bottle and then sits down across the table from me.

"Will you trade your life for hers?" Her voice is tight and she doesn't look at me.

"In a heartbeat, but if it comes to that I will be taking as many of them as possible with me."

It is a simple truth. Hell, I have been living on borrowed time ever single second since that Gun held a pistol to my head after killing the vampire that had enslaved me all those years ago. I was prepared to die as soon as I paid my penance, ever since the day the marks were put onto me. I have been dancing with death for a long time. All dances eventually end. It comes down to a simple plan.

I will survive if I can, I will die if I have to.

But, like I said I will be taking as many of them with me as I can possibly manage. No matter who or what they are.

Brain comes back carrying a small black duffle bag with him. He sits down and drinks his whiskey with the bag sitting at his feet.

"Go tend to your bar, we have things to discuss." He tells her flatly without even looking at her.

She gives him a wounded look that she covers up quickly. She nods at us briskly and leaves us alone.

"Did you get everything?"

"Yeah Joe, I fucking got everything." He tells me grimly.

"You up for this?" I ask him not because I really question the answer, more that I just need to hear it out loud.

He gives me a long look and then picks up the bottle and pours me another measure.

"Yeah Joe, I am up for this. You have trained me yourself. I will do what I have to do. You have been training me for something like this for a long time now." He tells me as he raises his glass in a toast.

"Yeah Brain, Happy Graduation Day." I tell him as we clink glasses and down our shots.

Hallmark once again has failed us by not making a card appropriate for an occasion such as this.

Screw Hallmark.

They suck.

CHAPTER THIRTEEN

Await further instructions, or rather stay tuned the voice had said, so we sat in Jenny's banquet room and waited. She left us alone, well we had each other and a bottle of Jamison's, so I guess we were in good company. Neither of us said much because there just really wasn't all that much to say.

After a couple of hours the phone rang again and without a word Brain hands it to me.

"Be at the north corner of the front yard of the last safe house you used, at darkfall. Come alone and unarmed." The same garbled voice as last time, only reason I could see for bothering to garble it was somebody was worried that I might recognize it.

Which meant that it was someone I knew.

Not a comforting thought.

But then again there were only two people in the world that I really trusted anyway and one was here drinking with me.

Didn't really want to think about where the other one might be and what might be happening to her.

The meet was set for darkfall, which meant that behind all of this was at least one vampire.

We only had a few hours to get ready, so I pushed all of the bullshit away and concentrated on the task at hand. Didn't matter who the voice on the phone was, didn't matter what vampire might be behind the whole thing, didn't matter what matter of conspiracy was going on. It didn't matter that even now, the Banshee inside of me were beginning to stir in their sleep. Right now, only one fucking thing mattered.

Getting Keela back.

Brain pulls a few things out of the bag and looks at me for instruction. His face is unreadable as he stands there.

"Do it!" I tell him as I pour one last drink for each of us.

When he is done we walk out of the banquet room just as Jenny is telling two uniformed cops that she hasn't seen us in days.

Crap.

Should have thought of it, should have known that a slaughter like that would make the news. What brought them looking for us, I didn't know but it didn't really matter. Maybe some player in the game thought that it would be cute to frame us for it. Maybe some random surveillance camera nailed us at the scene. Who knows? Like I said, it didn't really matter.

It was a tall thin rookie who barely looked old enough to shave but his partner was a rangy looking veteran with hard muscles and harder eyes. He looked at us and his hand went to his service pistol's holster unsnapping it.

The rookie beat him to it though, his gun was already out and pointed shakily at us.

"Freeze!"

Brain actually rolled his eyes at the kid and looked over at me to see how I wanted to play it.

"Left." I called it.

"Right." He acknowledged.

And just because we like to fuck with people, he went for the cop on the left and I went for the rookie on the right. It was a routine we had worked on out on patrol when there were two targets.

Confusion to our enemies.

I am on the rookie before he even registers that I moved. In one fluid motion I take his gun away and tap him upside his head. I am very careful to pull my punches on it, he is just a kid trying to do a job that he will grow into someday if nobody kills him first.

No need for him to die here today.

The kid goes down and he stays down and I turn to see how my partner in crime is doing.

Brain is in a mood and it isn't a gentle one.

The cop has his gun about halfway out of the holster when Brain forgoes all the moves I have taught him and decides to go all back alley and kicks him really damn hard in the balls. As the poor bastard folds, Brain tosses his gun into the trash can at the end of the bar and handcuffs him to the bar railing. The guy is a puddle of pain on the floor.

He never even put the damn duffle bag down.

It's early in the day and only a few hard core drunks are sitting at the bar shooting the shit and telling the usual lies. They have all stopped and are staring at us now. As are the few staff members on duty right now. Like is the case in most crisis's everyone is standing still waiting for someone else to do something.

Brain throws a couple of fifties on the bar and ignoring Jenny, he smiles at the cute young thing tending bar.

"Round for the house and please get the good officer here an icepack."

"Jesus Brian." Jenny voice sounds fragile and bruised and she is standing there with one hand on her stomach like she is going to be sick.

"Show is over friends. We return you now to your regularly scheduled programing. Carry on my wayward sons."

Then without a backward glance he walks out of the bar.

I walk up to Jenny and I gather her in for a hug. She deserves it no matter how things have worked out. She is good people and braver than she gives herself credit for. Not hard to do the math here kids, things are pretty damn over between her and Brain now if they weren't before.

I want to feel bad about that, really I do. It is just that there are so many damn other things that I have to feel bad about right now.

"Goodbye Jenny." I tell her softly.

And then I follow my friend out of the bar. He is waiting by the car with his arms cross and his face is a stone cold mask. This hasn't been an easy day, which is like, I suppose, the understatement of the fucking century.

The police are a complication but not a serious one. Not in the general fucked up scheme of things. Just one more thing to deal with as we move forward with what we are doing. As soon as we are gone someone will unlock the cuffs and the cop will call it in and we will have lots of eyes looking for us.   Cops take a fairly dim view of civilians beating the crap out of other cops so they will have a fairly big hard on for us.

All things considered though, they are really the least of our problems.

I look up at the sun as I walk over towards it and already it is starting to hang low in the sky. We have things to do and the clock is ticking and none of this shit matters right now.

I used to think that God hated me. That thought defined my existence and gave shape to my penance. Through loving Keela I have come to realize that God hates nobody and just like that I started to think of my penance as more of a service.

Maybe I was wrong.

Not about God hating me, but maybe what is to come is just part of the penance I owe. If so, well then so be it.

Like I said, none of this shit matters.

All that matters to me now is saving my girl and our child, everything and everyone else is secondary.

I walk towards my friend regretting the few seconds I just wasted thinking about all this shit.

CHAPTER FOURTEEN

I pull up in the Hummer that Brain insisted I take, I have always thought these fucking things looked ridiculous. Just to spite me I think the damn thing is neon yellow. It gets like a city block to the gallon and steers like a drunk whale.

And those are its good points.

Avanticus and his leather clad side kick Janelle are standing there holding Keela between them. She has a gag in her mouth and her hands are tied behind her back. There is a bruise on her cheek that causes rage to boil up in me and threatens to awaken the Banshee spirits and so I swallow my rage and put it away for the time being.

"Let her go." I tell him flatly as I step out of the monstrosity I drove there in.

"All in good time Black Irish, there are some…formalities to dispense with first." Avanticus tells us.

"Dispense away then motherfucker."

He stares at me for a long moment, doing his birdlike tilt of the head again, regarding me carefully.

"Very well then. Do you Black Irish freely agree to exchange your life for the life of this human female?" His tone is eager yet restrained.

"I do so, now cut her the fuck loose."

"Do you swear on your honor to freely exchange your life and not try to escape or attempt to kill us?" His tone is increasingly fevered.

I pull out my Highpoint and toss it away. Then I pull out my blade and toss it aside as well. I hold up my hands in the universal sign of surrender.

"I do so swear. Now let her the fuck go or no deal." I make my voice as flat and empty as I can.

He seems oddly uncertain and stares at me for a long moment before giving me a slow nod.

Janelle stands there as impassive as a statue, her posture rigid and she holds Keela like a sack of meat that she is completely indifferent to.

"Let her go." Avanticus orders.

She savagely rips the gag out of Keela's mouth and I flinched as I hear my girl gasp for air. The ropes around her wrists are the next to go.

Before she speaks, I gather force into my voice and weave into a slender thread of compulsion that if things weren't so damn dire I would never forgive myself for. It is a new talent and likely the result of carrying all of the Banshee within me.

And it is something for which she will never forgive me for.

"Walk away girl, don't look back."

Weakened as she is by her ordeal she succumbs easily to the compulsion I have just flung at her. She turns on her heel and marches away just as fast as she can. I watch her go knowing that she is crying and cursing me every damn step of the way.

Exactly five blocks from here we have arranged for one of Brain's company's interns to bring her to Brain. A large envelope of cash may or may not have been involved.

I want to feel a lot of things as I watch her walk away, God help me I do. I reach for it but it just isn't there. Not because I don't want it to be.

Simply because the sudden bone numbing relief that floods me leaves room for absolutely nothing else.

No matter what happens now I will count this as a win.

Probably the last one for tonight.

Avanticus draws his sword and runs a long pale finger down the glittery edge of it.

"So many things that I want to tell you, Black Irish. Such glorious tales. Despite the urgency that pulls at me I would not have you go to slaughter as ignorant as the sacrificial lamb. I would have you know why you are going to die tonight." His tone is dreamy and he is holding the sword reverently.

"Behold the sword, it is an ancient dark artifact from a civilization that vanished eons ago. I came across it in my travels centuries ago but have just recently started to understand what it is and what it does. As you know, vampires cannot wield magic but we can be affected by it. As I showed you one of your darkest fears the other night, it shows my kind our most reverent desire. Not only that, it shows us how to obtain it." He says as he takes a small step closer to me.

"And what did it show you?" He is going to tell me anyway, might as well ask and buy a little time.

"If I follow the instructions that the sword has laid out for me, I will bestow upon myself and my progeny the ability to walk in daylight. It will make me the head of the Council and give us vampires the edge we need to rule over you humans once and for all. You are simply the last piece of the puzzle, or rather the Banshee spirits you contain are. Once the sword has absorbed those energies it will have all it needs to grant me what I have so long desired" He says calmly.

Crap.

"And you will ruuuuule the world right? You might as well be twirling a mustache dude." I scoff at him.

For a moment he looks baffled, the ancients really don't do well with sarcasm. They simply don't get it.

"He mocks you, Master." Janelle tells him as she glares at me. Apparently she does get sarcasm.

"So that works out great for you fanged folk, why the hell are people in my Order fucking helping you? What the hell could you offer them to make them betray their own race?" I demand.

"Humans can always be bought or manipulated or both Black Irish. The Council has always owned an officer or two in your precious Order. It is just good business sense to do so. Your own female gave one a scratch last night much to his chagrin. Of course they don't know they are granting us the ability to walk in daylight, they aren't quite that corrupt. No, there is one that has helped me manipulate you here to this point that thinks that he is stopping a war, another which thinks that he is starting one. The Intervention follow orders, they were told that they should allow the gather of the Banshee but that under no circumstances was the rift to be reopened. They were ordered to use lethal force to ensure that no Adept talented enough to even try to open the rift survived. They followed those orders. Neither officer that we used is important now nor are their motivations." If he is angry at being mocked he doesn't show it but he does take another step towards me.

Really wish that he would stop doing that.

"Don't think Ennod is going to like your plan much. You ready to piss her off that badly?" My back is up against the car now, nowhere left to go.

A flicker of what might have been fear goes across his face and he fidgets nervously with the sword for a moment.

"Well, you saw what happened at the meeting to those who vex her as she likes to put it. Still by the time she learns of this it will be far too late. I will have the power to walk in daylight and to create other vampires who can. The council will support me and I will replace her as the head of it. What I offer is simply too valuable for them not to." He tells me but I can hear the faintest amount of uncertainty.

"Actually, they already know everything that you have just told me." I smile at him.

"That isn't possible Black Irish, really thought better of you than a silly bluff like that." He sneers.

"Not bluffing asshole, every single word that you have spoken has been broadcast to both selected members of my Order and Ennod's human servants. Not to mention, blasted all over the vamp nets. My friend Brain is very talented when it comes to gizmos and gadgets and he has me completely wired for sound." I open my leather jacket and show him the mike taped to my shirt.

Janelle moves first, in a heartbeat she is standing in front of me and then she tears the mike off of me. She crushes it in her fist and blurs back to stand by her Master.

"Does your word mean so little to you Black Irish? This gains you nothing by the time anyone can interfere with my plans they will be accomplished." Avanticus asks raising his sword.

"I have not broken my word, I have offered you no violence nor have I tried to escape. I have honored the terms of our agreement my life for the life of my woman. But there is something you should know, my friend Brain has made no such promises. He has made no promise not to try and kill you." I smile at him again.

Avanticus lowers the sword and takes a long look around him. He listens with his enhanced senses and I know he can't sense Brain.

"Your friend it would appear has decided not to join the party, Black Irish. It is just the three of us here right now, isn't that cozy? Now this has all been quite diverting and you have managed to stall rather effectively. You have succeeded in exposing me to both your Order and to my own Council, but in the scheme of things none of it will matter. I will feed the sword the energies in you, you will die knowing that your death enables me and mine to walk in daylight and that this ability will spell the doom of your race. The price tag for your little stunt will be knowing that your woman will live, you have traded your life for hers and I will honor that. But I have made no promises concerning your unborn child. Now, let us end this.

On your knees Black Irish time to die." He takes another step forward.

I start laughing and that confuses him once again. He looks over at his progeny and she gives him a small shrug. She doesn't know what the hell is so funny either.

"Agreed Avanticus it is indeed time to die. But I swore a long time ago that I would never kneel before anyone or anything ever again so we will all three die standing up if it is all the same to you." I tell him.

"No Black Irish, it is not all the same to me. The ritual requires that you kneel so kneel you shall. One last chance to do it yourself or I will simply have Janelle here force you to your knees and hold you there. Die with a little dignity human."

"Actually, Janelle will be the first one to die." I tell him calmly as I scratch my head.

Which was the signal that Brain has been waiting for as he sat with his favorite sniper rifle on the third level of a parking garage a little over a thousand yards away.

Well, it is one of the signals he has been waiting for any way.

The blessed explosive tipped .308 bullet takes her right between the eyes and at her age it is more than enough to tear most of her skull apart and send her convulsing in her death throes at her Masters feet.

I am so damn proud of him.

It was one hell of a shot.

Graduation day.

"YOU DARE!" Avanticus roars in shock and disbelief and it is that shock that buys me the seconds I need to go to stage two of the plan that my protégé and I came up with as we sipped decent Irish whiskey in Jenny's banquet room.

He is far too old to be taken out by a single rifle round, even a white phosphorus tip round wouldn't guarantee the job got done but what is to come next will.

We need to destroy him and the sword as thoroughly as possible, to be sure that his plan can never succeed. The information contained in the taped conversation we just broadcasted will allow Morton to clean house in The Order and hopefully restore it to something that the men and women who serve it can be proud of. Morton will be as brutal and ruthless as needed to get the job done and he will have Brain to help.

Ennod will do much the same in her own world but she will be far more brutal than Morton could ever be. She will weed out the dissenters on her Council root and stem and it will be a very long time before anyone has the nerve to conspire against her again.

If our plan works the Banshee threat will be removed and the balance will be restored. It is a win win for everyone.

Well, almost everyone.

I will have to die.

The Banshee sleep within me. If I die before they awaken, magical theory is that they will never awaken.

As I have said, I have been living on borrowed time for a very long time and now that time has simply run out.

Brain will take care of Keela and the baby. He had told me that once again after he had wired me for sound and yet one more time after he handed me the keys to the Hummer.

The Hummer that he loaded up with fifteen pounds of plastic explosives laced with white phosphorus and linked to the detonator that Brain right now holds in his hand.

That hand might tremble a little and he may openly weep as he does so but he is a full fledged Gun now and he will do what needs to be done.

He serves The Order. He has sworn to protect humanity at all costs.

Even this one.

So his hand may shake and he may weep but when I raise my hand he will push the red button and turn the spot that Avanticus and I are standing on into a fireball that for a few brief seconds will rival the heat of the sun.

I raise my hand and even though I know it is hopeless my training takes over and I make a hopeless attempt to survive.

I drop to the ground and roll under the Hummer.

Goodbye Keela.

I love you girl.

BOOM!

EPILOGUE

I walk through a seemingly endless gray nothingness towards a faint glimmering far off in the distance that I never get any closer to no matter how long I walk. I know somehow that I will never reach it. It feels like I have been walking forever, it feels like I will be walking forever. I remember nothing from before this grayness, just a faintly sorrowful feeling that I am walking away from all that I have known and loved. Each step is the reason for the one that follows, I walk without purpose. I walk because it is the only thing left to do. I walk because I simply have no idea how to stop.

Suddenly the grayness lifts and without transition I find myself in a dark wooded glade. I glance up and see an impossible amount of stars in the night sky as well as an impossibly huge full moon. It feels as if I should know this place, as if I have stood here before. Far off in the distance I think that I can hear the faintest echoes of ravens cawing.

I take a few more steps into the clearing and each step seems to stir memories within me, vague and undefined more fleeting impressions than real memories but more than I had before.

Then I see Her.

She sits on her throne created using the bones of long dead warriors, Her regal head bowed now in slumber. Her long red hair pooling into her lap.

Part of me knows that I knew her by name once but that is just the fading echo of a long ago whisper.

I stand before her for another eternity or two as a compulsion to touch Her builds within me.

When I can resist it no longer I reach out with one trembling finger and stroke her soft cheek.

Instantly She begins to crumble into a fine sparkling dust that a jasmine scented breeze scatters into the dark forest around us. I watch the dust blow away with no emotion that I can put words to.

A wave of unimaginable exhaustion crashes over me as the last of the dust twirls away into the night. A weariness that threatens to grind my bones and extinguish my very soul. A weariness that demands that I rest.

I gesture at the throne in distaste and before my eyes it slowly begins to transform. Bone is replaced by twisted branches and soft moss in every shade of green the world has ever known.

Opening my mouth I allow the burden I have been carrying, the burden that up to this very instant I have been unaware of, to spill forth onto the ground in front of the throne. That ground is now littered with small dully shining red stones. I knew what they were once but such knowledge is long gone from me now. My exhaustion leaves no room for musing on the matter.

I take one last long look around, at the forest, the moon, the stars and the throne that stands before me. The distant cawing of ravens seems slightly closer now. Memories try feebly to stab at me through the ever growing weariness flowing through me but they are in the end no match for it. The weariness pulls hard at me, one convulsive pull that ends my resistance to it.

I settle my weight onto the throne and I allow my eyes to slowly close. It is my time now to be still, my time now to rest, my time now to sleep.

To sleep.

Perchance to dream.

THE END

Once again we here at Alucard Press would like to give special thanks to the all great folks, staff and patrons alike at our local home away from home- THE PICKLED ONION in the Renton Highlands. Many of the words written in this and all three of the books were written at this fine establishment. Mind your pints!

We would also like to take a moment to thank each and every one of our Kickstarter backers who made it possible for us to bring THE BLACK IRISH CHRONICLES to a major pop culture convention and give the books some much needed exposure. Thanks people you are all rock stars in our eyes!

THE BLACK IRISH CHRONICLES

BLACK IRISH-Meet Joe Gunn
redeeming his soul one assassinated vampire at a time...

IRISH LULLABY- The
Dreamer has awakened...

IRISH CAR BOMB- Joe
Gunn and crew find themselves on the front lines of the Vampire/Banshee war...

THANKS FOR READING!

Made in the USA
San Bernardino, CA
15 March 2015